Jessica Souhami studied textile design at the
Central School of Art and Design.

In 1980 she formed Mme Souhami and Co., a travelling puppet company
using colourful shadow puppets with a musical accompaniment and a storyteller.

Her most recent titles for Frances Lincoln are *Mrs McCool and the Giant Cúchulainn*,
The Famous Adventure of a Bird-Brained Hen, *The Little, Little House* and *Sausages*.

Jessica works in collaboration with
book designer Paul McAlinden.

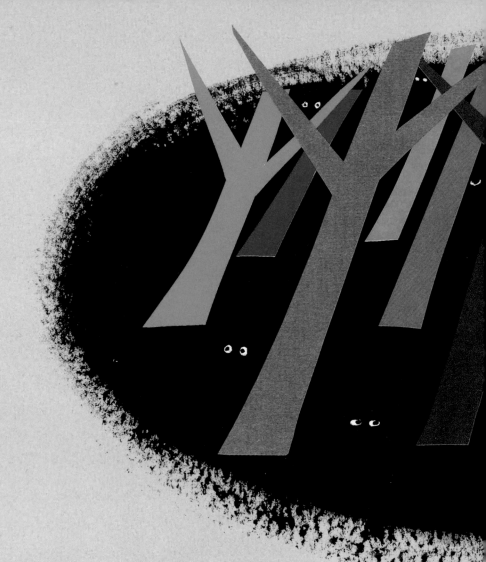

I'm going to tell you
a really spooky story,

so listen carefully to me…

In the dark, dark wood,
There was a dark, dark house,

Hoo-hoo-hoo!
Haa-haa-haa!

And in that dark, dark house,
There was a dark, dark room,

Hoo-hoo-hoo!
Haa-haa-haa!

And in that dark, dark room,
There was a dark, dark cupboard,

Hoo-hoo-hoo!
Haa-haa-haa!

And in that dark, dark cupboard,
There was a dark, dark shelf,

Hoo-hoo-hoo!
Haa-haa-haa!

And on that dark, dark shelf,
There was a dark, dark box,

Hoo-hoo-hoo!
Haa-haa-haa!

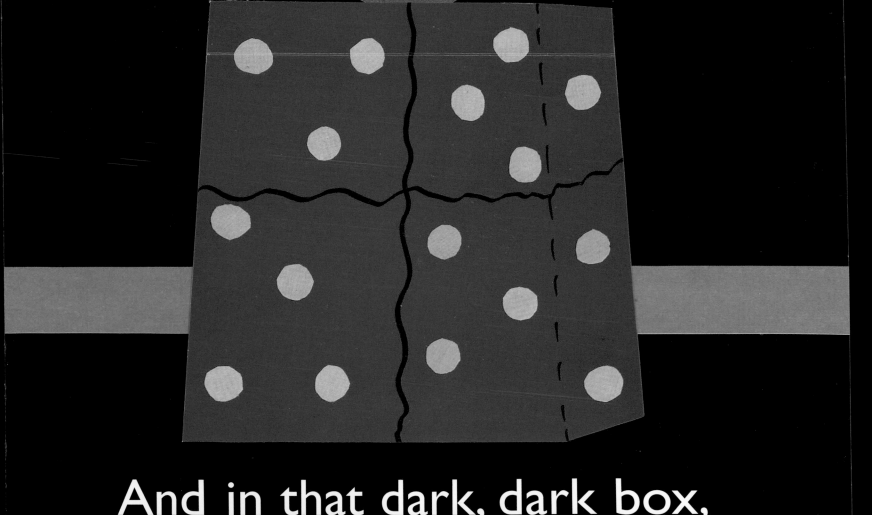

And in that dark, dark box,

MORE TITLES BY JESSICA SOUHAMI
FROM FRANCES LINCOLN CHILDREN'S BOOKS

SAUSAGES

When an elf rewards John's kindness with three wishes,
John and his wife start thinking of all the lovely things they could have.
But it is so difficult to choose and, as the hours pass,
John starts to feel hungry...

ISBN 978-1-84507-397-8

THE LITTLE, LITTLE HOUSE

Joseph and his family are so squashed and squeezed into their
little, little house that they can never be happy.
Can wise Aunty Bella solve their problem with the help of
six chickens, a rooster, a pretty brown cow and a very smelly goat?

ISBN 978-1-84507-108-0

THE FAMOUS ADVENTURE OF A BIRD-BRAINED HEN

Henny Penny is so bird-brained that when an acorn falls BOP!
on her head she thinks the sky must be falling in.
She sets off to see the king at once,
but Foxy Loxy isn't far behind and he is HUNGRY!

ISBN 978-0-7112-2026-3 (UK)
ISBN 978-1-84507-310-7 (US)

Frances Lincoln titles are available from all good bookshops.
You can also buy books and find out more about your favourite titles,
authors and illustrators on our website: www.franceslincoln.com